Rosa M. Curto / Aleix Cabrera

The fairies
tell us about...
Sharing

BARRON'S

The spring began to awaken lazily in the Forest of Dreams and the apple tree belonging to Keyla the fairy was in full bloom. "This year, it will surely bear fruit!" thought the fairy. "The tree is already quite big."

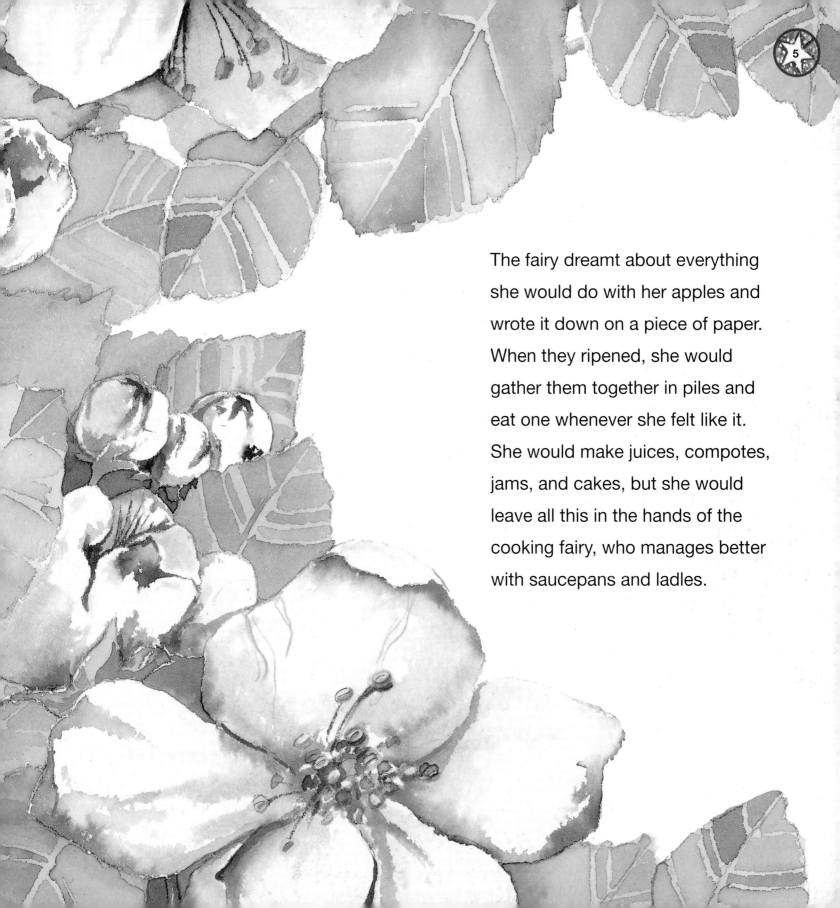

The fairy dreamt about everything she would do with her apples and wrote it down on a piece of paper. When they ripened, she would gather them together in piles and eat one whenever she felt like it. She would make juices, compotes, jams, and cakes, but she would leave all this in the hands of the cooking fairy, who manages better with saucepans and ladles.

Suddenly, she heard a crack-crack a bit higher up.
Keyla fluttered up to the treetop and found a pair
of little birds building a nest on a branch.
"What are you doing?" she asked them with a worried
look on her face. "Don't you know that you're ruining
the leaves? You'll spoil my harvest. Go away!"

The birds went to find another tree, without saying anything and the fairy breathed easy once again, as she gently touched the tender leaves of her apple tree. After a while, she heard another sound from below. Scratch-scratch!

A squirrel was scratching the bark non-stop to make a hideaway. The rest of the family was carrying loads of junk. They had come to stay and with so many holes... the apple tree was going to look like a piece of cheese!

"Go away!" shouted Keyla, angrily.
"If you continue to make holes in the trunk,
the apple tree will get sick and won't give
any fruit in the fall. Without any fruit,
there'll be no apple pie or juice."
So the squirrels packed their bags
and went away sadly.

Not even three seconds had gone by when the fairy heard yet another noise. Creak-creak. She glanced around and discovered what it was. Three of her friends were swinging happily from the branches.

"Three of you at the same time! No, you'll damage my apple tree!" shouted Keyla. "The game's over. It's my swing and from now on, I'll decide who gets on it." The three friends fluttered away toward the river bank, while Gossamer, the cooking fairy, picked plants near the trunk.

She pulled up sprigs of lavender, thyme, and rosemary.

When she noticed Keyla's distasteful glance,

she commented: "The pantry is empty and I'd like

to make a soup."

"Well, you'll have to eat something else. My apple tree

is very delicate and I don't want anyone to go near it."

None of the fairies had thyme soup for dinner. But this didn't bother Keyla because she had managed to stop everyone from touching her things. She swung happily, thinking about her apples and the great fall harvest.

However, this summer was never-ending,
because when you are alone, time passes
very slowly. Keyla had begun to miss
the games, the laughter, the bird's song,
and the buzzing of the bugs.

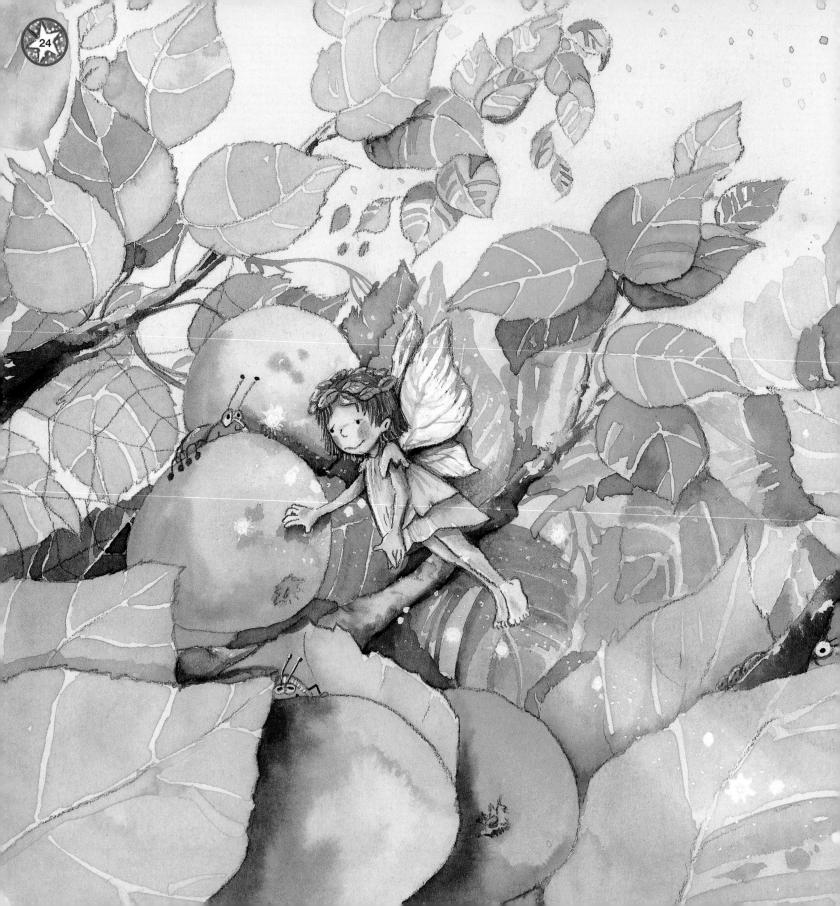

The apple blossom was transformed into ripe apples. In spite of this, the fairy felt sad and very lonely. It had been a long time since anybody had swung in her tree and now she had nobody to share her secrets, dreams, and apples with. She had been very selfish.

Without giving it any more thought, she fluttered her wings and
went to say sorry to everyone. Later, everyone had a party
to celebrate the harvest. Keyla was happy because she was once
again surrounded by smiles, music, and chatting. Apple pie
certainly tastes better when you have somebody to share it with.

Learning more

Fairy games

Air games

In the fall, the fairies plan wonderful air shows. They ride down to the ground on seeds and leaves, without using their wings. That's why the most important seeds are flat or umbrella shaped. Some fairies prefer to bounce down on the spider's webs as if they were little trampolines.

Water games

You'll rarely find a soaking wet fairy, but you will find them near water.

One of their favorite games is throwing flat stones so that they bounce over the calm waters of a pond. Those who haven't learned how to do it practice with stones of different sizes and shapes. Some even have jumping races.

Creative games

Creativity makes games endless for the fairies. They can make instruments to imitate animal sounds with anything. They use dry leaves, moss, flowers, and mushrooms to make wonderful songs.

Different types of seeds

Most plants, whether trees or herbs, are born from a seed. A seed is a kind of shell, called an embryo, which protects the plant before it develops.

There are a lot of different types of seeds. You'll see that if you look at some fruits and vegetables. Look at these examples.

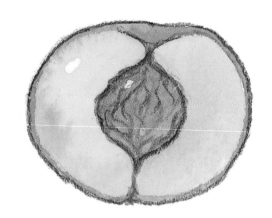

From the seed to the tree

The embryo remains asleep inside the seed until the time comes for the plant to grow. Then we say that the seed has germinated and the moment at which this takes place depends on each type of plant and on other things such as light, water, temperature, and the level of oxygen in the air. The root is the first part of the plant to come out, thanks to the food contained in the seed. The thin root grows under the ground to get water that feeds the rest of the plant. Little by little, a thin pale green, almost white stalk comes out from the top.

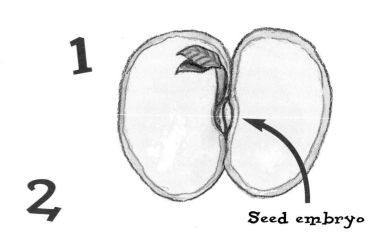

1

2

Seed embryo

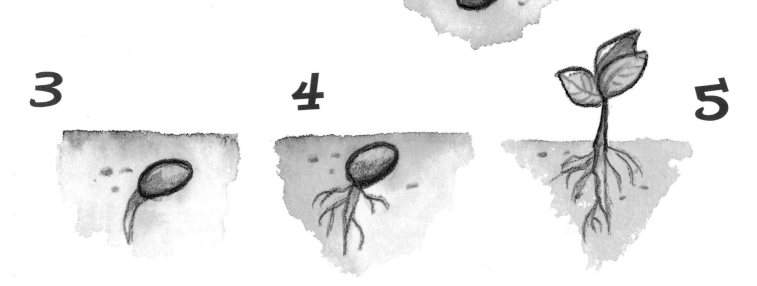

3

4

5

Then leaves and branches grow and the main stalk hardens until it becomes a trunk. The roots take in water and minerals for the whole life of the tree or plant, but this isn't enough to grow. The sunlight is the main source of energy and the plant uses its leaves to capture it. With the sun's energy, minerals, water, and air, the plant can make the things to help the stalk, leaves, flowers, and fruits to grow.

In time, the fruits grow in size and ripen. On the inside, the seeds are found, which could become new plants when they reach the ground — if the space has the right amount of water and sun. Then the cycle begins all over again.

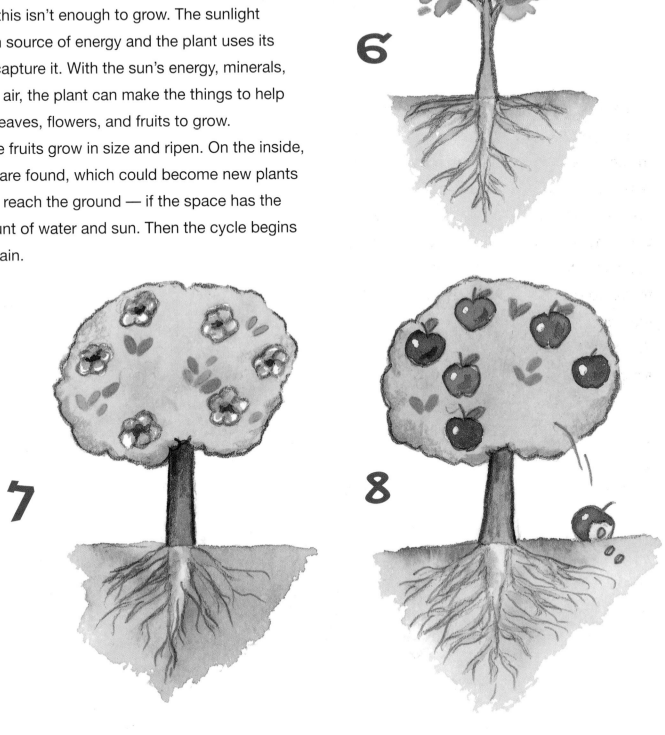

6

7

8

Sharing

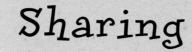

Sharing is the good feeling of giving without hoping to get anything in return — especially when you share with people who may not be your friends, and with those who have less than you. That's why some people also call it charity.

You are a sharing person when you...

Share your sandwich with somebody who has forgotten theirs.

Clean the house so that everyone feels comfortable.

Listen to a friend while he tells a problem to you.

A sharing act comes from your heart in a natural feeling and it means sharing anything, whether a toy or food – or your knowledge, time, and efforts.

For a sharing person, the act of giving comes from inside and he doesn't expect anything in return – not even a thank you.

You're not a sharing person if you...

Say "you owe me a favor," after you've helped somebody.

Expect everyone to notice you because of your deeds.

Do somebody else's job, without letting them learn how to do it themselves.

**The fairies tell us about...
Sharing**

Author: **Aleix Cabrera**
Illustrations: **Rosa M. Curto**
Design and layout: **Gemser Publications, S.L.**

First edition for the United States and Canada
published in 2010 by Barron's Educational Series, Inc.
Copyright © Gemser Publications, S.L. 2008
El Castell, 38 08329 Teià (Barcelona, Spain)

All inquiries should be addressed to:
Barron's Educational Series, Inc.
250 Wireless Boulevard
Hauppauge, New York 11788
http://www.barronseduc.com

ISBN-13: 978-0-7641-4377-9
ISBN-10: 0-7641-4377-8

Library of Congress Control No. 2009934886

Printed in China by L. Rex Printing Company Limited
Manufactured December 2009

9 8 7 6 5 4 3 2 1